D1324917

Split!

Written by
Jan Burchett and Sara Vogler

Illustrated by Paul Hess

CHAPTER ONE

Lia Vine scrambled up the tree trunk and clung desperately to a swaying branch. She could see the evil ground-dwellers below. She grasped a creeper in one hand, and fired deadly leaf bombs at her attackers with the other. Soon the ground-dwellers had all been defeated. They wouldn't be troubling her people again in a hurry. Lia had saved Skyville, the famous city in the trees.

I threw down my quill pen, picked up my story and dashed to the front of the class. This was the best thing I'd ever written. It had action, danger and gruesome villains – and I'd written it in ten minutes flat.

Miss Dordle, my teacher, looked at my work. She raised an eyebrow, sighed and slowly shook her head.

'This is far too exciting, Lia,' she said, fanning herself with a leaf.

'But you asked us to write about a perfect day, Miss Dordle,' I protested.

'How could that be your perfect day?' asked Miss Dordle patiently. 'Could you not have thought of something nice and steady for once? Barker wrote about counting tree knots, Fern says she would like to fold leaves and Buddy is writing a lovely description of watching dew dry.'

'But that's so boring!' I exclaimed.

'Nonsense,' said Miss Dordle. 'That is the Skyler way. Remember the Skyville motto, "Slow and safe". Swinging from branches indeed! Saving cities! And worst of all, you have dared to mention … the ground.' She looked round to make sure no one else had heard. 'How many times do I have to tell you? Good Skyler children do not talk about that place.'

'But our ancestors came from there,' I reminded her.

'True,' said Miss Dordle. 'Until the Split. Our noble ancestors split long, long ago from the dreadful creatures who lived down there – and live there still, I am sorry to say – then they climbed up here into the trees to make a new safe and steady life. And that is the end of it.'

'But the ground sounds so exciting. I'd love to know what it's really like,' I said.

My teacher went white, her nose quivered and her ears flapped with horror. 'Let us hear no more about it!' she squeaked.

I clumped back over the boring wooden floorboards to my boring wooden stool at my boring wooden desk. Miss Dordle was still looking at me. The end of her nose was drooping now, and her ears were flopping. I knew that look. It was the look that everyone in Skyville gave me. It was the look that meant, 'You are different from us, Lia. You are an oddbud.'

For the millionth time I wished our Skyville was like the Skyville in my stories. After all, we lived in a city built high in the trees, so you'd think we'd have rope swings, climbing races, secret hideouts and bold expeditions to see the people of the dark mysterious place below the leaves.

But no such luck. We Skylers were supposed to be content to live slowly and safely. Skylers never swung on ropes. Skylers never raced. Skylers wouldn't know a secret hideout if it sat on them. And Skylers wouldn't dream of venturing down through the leaves to that menacing place no one would tell me about.

But I did. I dreamt of nothing else.

When we'd all finished, Miss Dordle showed us a piece of bark with a message carved on it. It looked important.

'Prepare your ears for some news, children,' she said. Everyone obediently held out the tops of their ears. 'The Great Skyville Feast is to take place soon,' she continued, 'and Mayor Crabapple would like you lucky children to make twig decorations for the dinner tables!'

Everyone clapped. I groaned.

'The feast is so special,' said Miss Dordle, 'that we only dare hold it every twelve years, once every twelve tree-rings.'

This sounded interesting. I flapped my hand in the air. 'Which day will it be, Miss Dordle? Can we go?'

'Not so hasty, Lia. The Elders will hold a meeting to decide when to have a meeting to decide the date. And of course children are not allowed ...'

I flapped my hand again. 'What happens at the feast?' I interrupted.

'At the feast we celebrate the day long

ago when our ancestors first climbed up to this happy place.'

'Will there be stories about the gr ... the place we don't mention?'

'Yes ... I mean, no ... I mean ... it need not concern you, Lia,' said Miss Dordle, fluttering her hands anxiously. 'Get out your willow branches, everyone. It is time for catkin-counting.'

So there *would* be stories about the ground at the Great Skyville Feast! Suddenly I wanted more than anything to go.

After school, I burst into our house, making our whole tree sway and the shutters clatter. Mum clung to the rafters for support and Dad dropped his leaf weaving.

'There's going to be a feast!' I shouted, dancing round our tree trunk. 'The Great Skyville Feast!'

'Steady on, Lia,' said Dad, as he slowly bent down to pick up his weaving.

'I can't wait,' I squeaked.

'How many times do I have to tell you, Lia,' sighed Mum, lowering herself into a chair. 'Slow and calm will bring no harm. Hasty and quick will make you sick.'

'I'm never sick, Mum,' I exclaimed. 'And this is so exciting!'

'Exciting?' said Dad, his ears flapping with worry. 'I do hope not. The last time someone got excited at the feast they ended up with a splinter ...'

'Never mind that,' I interrupted. 'The important thing is – which robe should I wear?'

'Not so fast, Lia ...' Mum began.

'I can't wait to hear the stories about the ground, and the people there and why the Skylers split from them,' I interrupted.

There was a horrified silence. Finally my mother spoke.

'There are things talked about at the feast that are for the ears of grown-ups only,' said Mum. 'And I'm afraid you are not old enough to go.'

'But that's not fair!' I shouted.

'But that is how it is,' said Mum, patiently. 'You cannot go to the feast.'

'That's what you think,' I said to myself.

CHAPTER TWO

Finally, after weeks of meetings and discussions to decide the date, it was the day of the Great Skyville Feast.

Mum and Dad were taking all morning to decide where to stick the last leaf on Mum's headdress. I sat miserably in my bedroom wondering how I could get to the feast.

Then an idea wiggled into my brain, like a caterpillar burrowing into an apple. I flung open the doors of my cupboard, rummaged among the rubbish and pulled out a ball of twine, my old leaf collection, and my junior woodwork kit.

Ten minutes and a bandaged thumb later, I stood staring into the mirror. A strange figure stared back. It was wearing a long robe, a leafy sort of hat which covered its face – and it was as tall as a grown-up. I couldn't believe it was me! My disguise was brilliant.

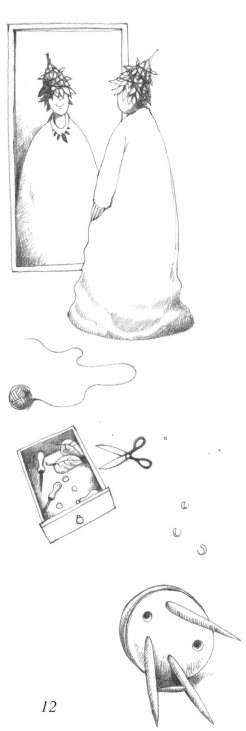

I'd stuck some leaves on a bit of twine for a headdress, 'borrowed' Mum's second-best robe and turned two of the legs of my extra-safe five-legged stool into posts to walk on. I decided to call them my Sticks That Imitate Long Tall Skylers, or STILTS for short. When I strapped them to my feet, they made me as tall as my dad. I looked like an adult.

After tea, I paced up and down my bedroom as the sun set and the glow-worm lamps lit up over Skyville. I couldn't wait till it was time to go to the feast. I had my disguise ready under my bed and a bubbly feeling in my stomach – as if a swarm of ants were having a wild party in it.

The giant sloth went by, hanging upside down from a branch and moving slowly along, hand over hand. Skylers in their best robes were sitting on his stomach. They were off to the feast – that is, if the sloth went the right way. That was the trouble having a sloth for a bus. You never knew if he was going to stop or turn left or curl up and have a sleep. But he was our only transport and he was slow and safe.

Mum and Dad came ambling up to say goodbye.

'The childwatcher will be by to check on you,' said Dad.

'Do not do anything silly, Lia,' said Mum solemnly. 'Remember, safe and sure will keep you secure. Bold and bad …'

'… will drive me mad. Yes I know, Mum.'

The only thing driving me mad at the moment was my parents hovering about.

The moment the front door closed, I arranged my pillow and my toy sloth under my bedclothes so it looked as if I was asleep. That should fool the childwatcher when she came past and stuck her mirror on a stick up to my bedroom window to check on me.

The walkway was empty as I stepped out of my door, wearing my robe and headdress. Clutching my stilts and glow-worm torch in my hand, I scampered along towards the Central Skyville Superdrome.

The Central Skyville Superdrome may sound grand but in the boring Skyler way it was just like our houses only ten times bigger, built round four trees, and with a nameplate. There were three pears and a pine cone stuck over the entrance. The mayor and the Elders had spent days putting those up.

Mayor Crabapple stood in the doorway, greeting the guests. I hid in the shadows and put on my stilts. I wished I'd practised with them because I found they were almost impossible to walk on. And I could hardly see a thing through my headdress. I fumbled my way round the walls until I reached the entrance. Now all I had to do was stand up straight and glide in, like any other grown-up.

I let go of the doorway, and wobbled into the Superdrome.

'Well, well, well!' said Mayor Crabapple. 'Who have we got hiding under here?'

CHAPTER THREE

I stood stock still, hardly daring to breathe.

'I would know that face anywhere!' the mayor went on. 'Mrs Larch, is it not! Nice headdress – if a little overdone! Welcome to the feast.'

'Thank you, your Firship,' I murmured. I'd got away with it!

Inside the Superdrome, Skylers were milling about a huge banqueting hall. I spotted Mum and Dad on the other side of the room, talking to our neighbours, the Spruces. I had to find a place to lie low until the stories started.

Clinging to chairs and tree trunks, I
wobbled round the room towards the
food table and collapsed into a chair,
next to Barker's table decoration – two
twigs in a lump of resin. I reached over
to a plate of stuffed acorns and crammed
three into my mouth.

'Lia Vine?'

I nearly choked. Someone must have
recognised me. But nobody was looking
my way. There was a small group
whispering in a huddle nearby. I pulled
out my ears to listen.

'Yes. That child is so bold.'

'I caught her skipping the other day!'

'And those stories she writes!'

'What an oddbud!'

'Just like her Great-uncle Runnicles – and he came to a bad end!'

I helped myself to a jellied conker and pulled out my ears a little more. Who was Great-uncle Runnicles? I was just wondering what bad end he'd come to when Mayor Crabapple politely tapped the table for silence.

'Fellow Skylers,' he announced solemnly, 'we are gathered at the Great Skyville Feast to tell stories of our ancestors. Prepare your ears for the tale of the Split.'

There was a soft murmuring and some hand flapping and everyone held on to their ears. I'd never seen the Skylers this excited!

'Many moons ago, when this forest was young, our ancestors lived below the leaves. They lived on … the ground.' There was a shudder of horror from the audience. I was delighted. At last I was going to find out what I wanted to know.

Suddenly there was a commotion at the door and the crowd parted to reveal Mrs Sycamore from the corner shop. She was in a terrible state. Someone led her to the only spare chair – right next to me. I kept my headdress well over my face. I didn't want her recognising me. I was always in her shop buying sugared sticky buds.

'I am in such a flutter,' she said loudly to the whole Superdrome. 'Something terrible has happened.'

What was that, I thought. Was a caterpillar going too quickly across a walkway? Had the sloth picked his nose? The Skylers waited patiently while Mrs Sycamore mopped her brow with some moss.

'I was quietly hanging my underwear on my washing branch to dry,' she said, 'when the branch snapped off before my very eyes!' Skyler ears began to flap nervously.

'Are you certain, Mrs Sycamore?' asked the mayor.

'Quite certain, your Firship. It went over the garden wall – and took my undergarments with it!'

Mr Green from the leaf mould factory flapped a worried hand. 'Pardon me, your Firship, but I have had three branches and a twig go in the last week,' he said. 'They dropped straight through the leaves and disappeared. And it was my favourite twig.'

'There are no buds on my tree,' called an anxious voice from the back of the crowd.

'And our ivy is dying,' called another.

There was a long silence. Then the mayor took a deep breath.

'It seems,' he announced, 'that something is happening to our precious trees – the very foundation of our city. And I think we all know who is responsible.'

There was a horrified murmuring. So many ears were flapping it was setting up a breeze.

'It can only be the evil creatures we split from all those tree-rings ago. The creatures that live on … the ground.'

I held out my ears till they hurt, trying to find out more. The crowd was muttering quietly.

'Living down there in the gloom with their nasty little ways.'

'We all knew they would do something to us one day.'

'We must not tell the children.'

'Fellow Skylers,' said the mayor importantly. 'Let us not panic. There will be no stories tonight. The Elders and I must arrange a meeting to decide what to do about this terrible news.'

The crowd sighed with relief and started chatting again. I couldn't believe it! Our trees would have all fallen down by the time the Elders had worked out what to do. Didn't anyone else understand? I wanted to warn them, there and then, but I knew it was no good. They wouldn't listen, and I'd just get into big trouble for sneaking into the feast. I'd be more of an oddbud than ever.

I got to my feet and made straight for the door, stumbling against people as I went. I was nearly there when I bumped into a tree trunk and my headdress fell back from my face. Suddenly everyone was looking at me.

'Is that a child? She should not be here.'

'Did she hear anything unpleasant?'

'Come back, child!'

But there was no way I was going to stop now. As the Skylers moved slowly forwards I threw myself at the door.

The moment I was out of the Superdrome I kicked off my stilts and robe, and headed for the shadows. I knew what I had to do. I wasn't scared of any old ground-dwellers. I would save Skyville just like I had in my story. And no one would call me Lia the Oddbud any more.

I tucked my robe into my knickers and gripped my glow-worm torch in my teeth. There was nothing for it. It was up to me to find out what was going wrong with our trees. I'd have to go down. I took a deep breath and jumped for the nearest tree.

I landed safely. Clinging tightly to a bunch of leaves, I shone my torch down into the darkness. I could see another branch below. I began to climb down.

After a while I couldn't see Skyville any more. My tree seemed to have run out of branches so I swung across to the next one. But this tree felt different – the bark was dry and crumbly under my fingers.

Suddenly I heard a creaking sound and my branch shuddered and lurched alarmingly. Then, with a horrible crack, it broke under me and I plummeted through the leaves.

CHAPTER FOUR

The next thing I knew I was lying on the ground. I'd lost my torch and everything was pitch black.

Then there was a groaning sound from under me and the ground shook and heaved, sending me sprawling. I rolled on to my back and looked up, ready to face an evil ground-dweller.

A boy stood over me holding a glowing lantern. He was about my age, he was wearing very odd clothes and he didn't look pleased to see me.

'Are you trying to kill me?' he shouted. 'First I'm covered in falling knickers and now you land right on top of me – and I was asleep!' He thrust his lantern in my face. 'You're a tree-person! We've heard stories about you lot.'

'I'm a Skyler, actually,' I said, struggling to my feet. It was weird standing on the ground. It was solid and it didn't sway. I felt sick. 'And I didn't mean to squash you,' I went on, trying to keep my balance. 'I was climbing down and I fell and you just got in the way. It was an accident.'

'And I suppose it's just an accident that you tree-people keep chucking branches down,' said the boy crossly. 'It's been raining wood for days.'

I could see the ground was covered in dead leaves and broken bits of tree.

'It's not us,' I protested. 'The evil ground-dwellers who live in the forest have damaged the trees. If you take my advice you'll get out of here. They sound nasty.'

'Load of rubbish!' said the boy. 'They're not called ground-dwellers, they're Rootles, and they're not evil.'

'How do you know?' I demanded.

'Because I'm one,' he said grimly. 'And we don't damage trees. We leave that to you lot.'

I looked at the trees in the lantern light. Bark was hanging off the trunks in strips and the wood underneath looked shrivelled. The lower branches had all snapped off. These trees didn't look strong enough to be holding up Skyville. They were dying.

'Listen, ground-dweller,' I said. 'Why would we damage the trees? If they die, that's the end of Skyville. And it'll be the end of the Rootles too. It won't be just a few branches falling on your head, you'll have the school, the Superdrome, the shopping centre, several hundred houses and a lot of Skylers dropping on you. Not to mention the giant sloth!'

At that moment there was a cracking sound above our heads. I leapt forward and gave the boy an almighty shove, sending him sprawling.

'What do you think you're ...?' he spluttered.

A huge branch thundered to the ground – just where we'd been standing. The boy looked at the branch. Then he looked back at me.

'Thanks,' he muttered.

'Are you convinced now?' I said. 'If us Skylers were trying to hurt you ground-dwellers, would I have bothered to save you?'

'Suppose not. But stop calling me ground-dweller. My name's Sprout.'

'And I'm Lia,' I said.

We stood for a moment shuffling our feet in embarrassment.

'If it's not your people,' I said at last, 'and it's not my people, why's it happening?'

'I don't know,' said Sprout. 'My dad's chief Rootle. I suppose we'd better speak to him. Although he never listens to me. No one ever does. That's why I came out here. To get away from them all. They just rush around all the time and say I do everything too slowly and I think about things. They call me oddbud.'

'That's what the Skylers call me!' I exclaimed. 'Come on. We've nothing to lose. Let's go and see him.'

Sprout strode quickly through the forest. I couldn't believe the Rootles thought he was slow. I'd never met anyone who walked faster than me before. I had a good look at him as we went along. He was a bit like a Skyler, except that his hands were round and stubby and his ears didn't flap or flop but kept moving as if picking up distant sounds. His clothes were different too.

Skylers wore robes, but this boy had a short tunic and a funny garment that wrapped round each leg.

I pestered him with questions as we went along.

'Do you have schools down here?'

'Course we do!' he snorted. 'But I wish we could be there for longer.'

'Isn't eight hours long enough?' I gasped.

'Eight hours? We only do three spellings and two minutes of mental maths. Then we go home.'

'Lucky you,' I said. 'What do you do for the rest of the day?'

'We play all the usual games,' he said. 'Hop, skip and dash, six-card-snap, leap-before-you-look. But by the time I've started everyone else has finished.'

'It's better than leaf-matching,' I laughed. 'That takes all week!'

We came into a huge clearing lit by hundreds of lanterns. There were strange buildings all over the place made of lumps of grey stuff piled up on each other.

Although it was now late
at night, hundreds of squat Rootles were
still working or scuttling about, heads
poking forwards. They were dressed like
Sprout but moved much faster than him.

'This is Rootstock,' said Sprout. 'It's
where us Rootles live.'

'Your houses are weird!' I exclaimed.
'They're not wooden!'

'Course not,' scoffed Sprout. 'They're
made of rocks.'

He led the way to the largest house. A man came rushing out of the opening and nearly knocked me flying. He was wearing a metal band on his head with stones stuck on it. He stopped short when he saw Sprout.

'So you're back, son,' he said sharply. 'Decided not to sulk in the forest after all.'

'Didn't want to come back,' muttered Sprout. 'Not after you all moaned at me for taking more than thirty seconds to finish my tea. But I found this tree-person ... I mean Skyler. Her name's Lia.'

The chief Rootle circled me so quickly that my sick feeling came back. 'Tree-people aren't welcome here!' he shouted, his ears bristling.

More Rootles came over, jostling and chattering.

'Trust that oddbud to find a tree-person.'

'They're the ones that caused the Split!'

'We had one here once.'

'He came to a bad end.'

'Tree-people are evil.'

'Tree-people throw branches.'

'Listen, Dad,' said Sprout urgently. 'Lia says it's not the Skylers throwing things. The trees are dying. Skyville will fall on us if we don't get together with them and sort it out!'

But nobody took any notice. Soon there were Rootles all around me, poking sharp fingers in my ribs and muttering angrily in my ears.

'Nasty tree-person!'

'Don't want her here with her wicked ways!'

'Sent 'em packing all those years ago!'

All I could see were angry faces. I turned and ran. But I didn't get very far. Quick, impatient hands grabbed me and dragged me out of the clearing. They took me deeper and deeper into the dark forest. At last we stopped in front of a cage. I was pushed into it and the door was slammed shut with a resounding clang.

'Dad!' protested Sprout. 'She's done nothing wrong.'

'And she won't be able to while she's stuck in there.' Sprout's dad took him by the scruff of the neck. 'You're coming with me, my lad.'

They disappeared into the darkness.

I grasped the bars of my prison cage. I sat down on the cold floor with my head in my hands, in the pitch dark. Things were not going according to plan. The Lia in my stories would never have ended up falling out of a tree and being put in a cage, like a parrot.

And then I heard heavy footsteps coming through the leaves towards me.

CHAPTER FIVE

'Blithering blossoms!' said a voice. 'A Skyler in a cage!'

There stood a man with glowing lamps stuck on his forehead, arms and round his neck. He wore a short, ragged Skyler robe and on his legs he had the strange garment of the Rootles. His hair was wild, his ears twitched excitedly and there was a broad grin on his face. He flapped a friendly hand at me.

'Fancy seeing another Skyler below the trees!' he said. 'Didn't think they had it in them. Runnicles Juniper at your service.'

'Are you my Great-uncle Runnicles?' I gasped. 'Everyone says you came to a bad end.'

'Do they?' said Great-uncle Runnicles, beaming. He looked himself up and down, sending ripples of light over his odd clothes. 'I think they must be wrong. I'm very much alive. But it's nice to hear they still talk about me. You must be my soppy niece Magnolia's daughter. I suppose you fell down here.'

'No I didn't!' I said indignantly. 'I climbed down. Well, most of the way.'

'Good show, great-niece. You're a chip off the old block and no mistake. Not like the others – spineless bunch of namby-pambies. Never got on with them. Decided to leave and explore the world. So I slipped off down here one day when no one was looking. What's your name, girl?'

'Lia. And I'm here to find out what's wrong with the trees, so if you could just let me out …'

'What is wrong with the trees?'

'They're dying!'

'Pickled pine cones! Are they really?'

'We have to do something,' I said. 'Or the whole of Skyville will fall and flatten Rootstock. So could you let me out of here …?'

But Great-uncle Runnicles was thinking hard. 'I have an idea,' he announced. 'Come and stay with me. There aren't any trees above my house so we'll be safe when it happens.'

'But what about everyone else?'

'Good point,' said Great-uncle Runnicles. He rubbed his chin. 'I know – we'll get the Rootles to stand on each other's shoulders and hold Skyville up. That should do the trick!'

'But they won't agree to that!' I protested.

'Good point,' said my great-uncle. 'They're not very cooperative. Never did get on with them. Better think again.'

'While you're thinking,' I said irritably, 'perhaps you could …'

'Lia!' called a voice. 'Lia!'

Sprout came running out of the shadows, looking anxiously behind him. He stopped short at the sight of my great-uncle.

'Galloping greenfly! The forest is busy tonight,' exclaimed Great-uncle Runnicles, shining one of his lights at him. Then his face fell. 'Oh, it's a Rootle.'

'This is Sprout, Uncle Runnicles,' I said. 'He's not like the others.'

'Hope not!' said Great-uncle Runnicles, grinning. He flapped a hand at Sprout. 'Runnicles Juniper at your service.'

'Runnicles Juniper!' exclaimed Sprout. 'My dad's told me all about you. He said you came to a bad end years ago.'

'Fizzling fungus!' said my great-uncle. 'All I did was try to improve the Rootle lighting system. Not my fault the whole thing exploded. I made my escape under cover of the smoke. I didn't think they'd listen to my explanation.'

'Rootles don't listen to anyone,' said Sprout bitterly, 'especially an outsider. I'm in big trouble – for making friends with a Skyler.'

'In case you'd forgotten,' I shouted crossly, 'that Skyler happens to be stuck in a cage!'

'Why didn't you say so?' said my great-uncle cheerfully. 'Now, how shall we open it?'

Sprout pulled a key from his pocket. 'I took this while no one was looking,' he said. He unlocked the cage door and I scrambled out. 'I'll be in even more trouble when they find out! They mustn't catch us here.'

'I've just hatched a jolly good idea,' said Great-uncle Runnicles. 'We'll beetle off to my house and make …'

I pulled out my ears. Maybe this time he did have a useful plan.

'… a really good breakfast.'

CHAPTER SIX

Breakfast sounded like a great idea. I was starving. It was hours since I'd eaten that jellied conker.

'Come on then,' said Great-uncle Runnicles. 'We've got quite a walk ahead of us.' He twisted a button on his tunic and all his lights went out. 'Won't be wanting these,' he said as we set off.

Sprout looked doubtful. 'But we always need lights in the forest,' he said, holding up his lantern.

'The sun will be up by now,' said Great-uncle Runnicles, 'and we'll be out of the forest soon.'

'Out of the forest!' Sprout and I gasped together.

'Of course.' Great-uncle Runnicles pointed ahead. 'Look!'

We stopped in astonishment. There were no more trees. The sun was coming up over a huge open space, covered in little green plants with thin leaves that pointed to the sky.

'Skylers never go out of the forest,' I said. 'They wouldn't dare.'

'Neither do Rootles,' said Sprout nervously. 'It was something that happened out there that caused the Split.'

'What was it?' I gasped.

Sprout shook his head. 'No idea.'

'No one seems to remember,' said Great-uncle Runnicles. 'It was such a long time ago. Now, see those hills in the distance? My house is just below them.'

'And what's beyond the hills?' I asked eagerly as we followed my great-uncle through the strange green plants.

Sprout looked back at the forest every now and then, his ears twitching nervously. 'I expect you've been everywhere, seeing as you're an explorer.'

'Not exactly everywhere,' said Great-uncle Runnicles, going a bit pink. 'Got a bit too settled in my little home with no one to bother me. But I certainly intend to one day. When I get round to it. Maybe next leaf-budding. Now look lively, children. There's my house.'

Great-uncle Runnicles' house was a tiny wooden shack held together with bits of rope. It was more falling down than standing up. Great-uncle Runnicles dragged open the rickety door and led us inside. The shack was dark and cramped. There was a bed at the far end, a couple of home-made armchairs next to a glowing wood fire and curious objects scattered all over the place. The

Skylers would have shuddered to see such a mess.

'Don't mind my inventions,' said my great-uncle as we tried to find a place to sit. 'Now, on with breakfast.'

He took a round brown object with a rough crust out of a cupboard.

'Try some of this,' he said as he sliced off a piece. 'I invented it using the seeds that grow on the hills. It's my Big Round Edible Dough – bred for short.'

The bred was as tough as old bark, even when it was spread with some crushed berries which Great-uncle Runnicles called Just A Mouthful of Mush.

Sprout and I sat by the fire. I was amazed how fast Sprout gobbled down his bred and jamm. While we ate, we thought of ways to save the trees. Great-uncle Runnicles made several suggestions, the last one involving a walking stick, a flock of pigeons and a kettle. We weren't getting anywhere.

'What we have to do,' said Sprout, slurping down some bitter root juice, 'is find a way to bring back life to the trees.'

'Life to the trees …' said Great-uncle Runnicles thoughtfully. 'Leaping leafspot! That reminds me of a story in a dusty old book I found when I was a child in Skyville. I've got it here somewhere.'

He started rummaging under the bed. 'In fact it was the only book I ever found in Skyville. I made sure no one caught me reading. They thought I was an oddbud – and reading stories was a very dangerous thing to do, according to the Skylers.'

But I wasn't listening any more. For the first time since I'd arrived in Rootstock I was feeling sleepy. It was warm by the fire and my head nodded as Great-uncle Runnicles started to read.

I woke up with a snort. I couldn't think where I was. Then I remembered. I had a quest. I was going to save the trees. The Lia in my stories wouldn't have sat around chewing tough old bred and falling asleep in the middle of her adventure. Sprout was snoring his head off and my great-uncle was still reading.

'... and the Waterfall of Wonderful Wetness tumbled down the rocks into a great river which flowed across to the forest and gave life to the trees. If ever it stopped flowing, the bark would peel, the branches would fall and the trees would die …'

'That's it!' I yelled.

'That's what?' asked Great-uncle Runnicles, his ears flapping with surprise.

'The answer!'

Sprout opened his eyes and looked around wildly.

'I've found out something important while you've been asleep,' I told him.

'Wasn't asleep. Just resting my eyes.'

'You and I have to leave,' I said, 'and straight away.'

'Leave?'

'It was in the story!' I exclaimed. 'The Waterfall of Wonderful Wetness – whatever that is – brings life to the trees. I never knew trees needed water to live!'

'Nor did I,' said Sprout, as we peered at Great-uncle Runnicles' book. 'The only water we have is rainwater. Never heard of this waterfall. And I've never seen a river in the forest.'

Next to the story
was a faded drawing
of a huge wall of
water pouring
down a
rock face.
Rain never
came down like
that in Skyville,
even during a
storm. The water
wove its way across the
land and into the distance
where the trees of our forest
stood.

'There must be something wrong with the waterfall,' I said. 'We've got to find it!'

'Are you sure we should do this?' asked Sprout nervously. 'What if it's dangerous?'

'It'll be more dangerous when Skyville lands on your head,' I told him. 'We have to go.'

'I'll pack my travel trolley!' exclaimed Great-uncle Runnicles.

And he produced a large wooden box on wheels with a stick for a handle. He chucked in a selection of weird gadgets, then he added three breds, a pot of jamm and the storybook.

'Perhaps Sprout and I should go on our own,' I said hurriedly.

'Nonsense, my girl,' said Great-uncle Runnicles. 'You'll get lost without me.'

CHAPTER SEVEN

We were completely lost – thanks to Great-uncle Runnicles. We'd been travelling for hours with only bred and jamm to keep us going. My great-uncle had insisted on using his way-finding invention – a twig on a stick. He said that when he spun it, the twig would always end up pointing the way to go. Pulling his travel trolley behind him he had led us up the hills, into a clump of prickly plants and through a thicket of pine trees. Then we'd clambered over a huge area of jagged rocks that seemed to go on for ever, waiting every five minutes for Great-uncle Runnicles whose trolley wheels kept getting stuck in the gaps.

'We've been past this rock three times,' moaned Sprout. 'We're going round in circles.'

'Not at all, my boy,' beamed Great-uncle Runnicles. 'I'll soon find the right way with my peeperscope.' He sat down next to his trolley, rummaged amongst

his inventions and pulled out a long thin box with a hole at each end. He peered through it. 'Boggling bark beetle!' he exclaimed. 'There's a dark cave ... with hair growing over it!'

'You're looking at Sprout's ear, Uncle Runnicles,' I sighed.

'Silly me!' he said. 'Wait a minute – what's this? Four small hills and one big one.'

'That's your foot,' groaned Sprout.

'So it is.'

'We can't hang around here all day!' I said impatiently as Great-uncle Runnicles scanned the horizon. 'We've got to get going.'

'Slow down!' said Sprout. 'We don't know which way. You sound like a Rootle!'

'And you're being a Skyler,' I scoffed.

We glared at each other for a moment. Then we both giggled.

'What about a quick think, then we set off,' I suggested.

'Okay,' said Sprout. 'This waterfall must start somewhere high so the water can actually fall.'

'You're right,' I said. 'Somewhere steep like in the picture.'

'The only high place I can see,' said Sprout, 'is over there.'

There was a huge, grey wall of rock in the distance.

Great-uncle Runnicles pointed his peeperscope at it.

'I thought that was a molehill!' he said. 'Silly me. The peeperscope's the wrong way round.'

We set off towards it. As we got nearer, the rock towered above us. We walked along at its base, searching for telltale drips of water.

Then we came to a place with steep, green-stained walls and, at our feet, a huge dip scooped out of the rock. I stopped dead.

'This is it,' I announced. 'This is the Waterfall of Wonderful Wetness.'

'How do you know?' said Sprout crossly. 'You haven't even looked properly.'

'I know because …'

'It's not like the picture,' said Great-uncle Runnicles. 'Where's all the water?'

'You're being hasty again, Lia,' warned Sprout.

I pointed to a wooden sign with faded, old-fashioned writing on it. 'Read this,' I said.

There was another sign behind. We read it.

HERE IS THE

WATERFALL
~ OF ~
# WONDERFUL
# WETNESS

<u>PLEASE</u>

BE CAREFUL THAT YOU DO NOT
SLIP OR GET WET OR SHOUT
OR MAKE WAVES OR JUMP
IN A SILLY FASHION OR THROW
STONES OR GO FOR A SWIM OR
GET SWEPT AWAY OR LEAVE
LITTER

'You win,' said Sprout. 'But where's the water?'

'I don't know,' I said. 'Maybe that's the problem – it's dried up.'

'It proves one thing,' said Sprout. 'The Rootles and the Skylers both knew about the waterfall once. And they didn't get on even then!'

'We've got to get to the top,' I said, gathering up my robe. 'Come on.'

Great-uncle Runnicles looked doubtfully at the rock and spun his twig.

'The twig says this way!' he announced, pointing along the bottom of the rock. 'And that's the way I'm going. Look after my trolley.'

And before we could stop him he'd disappeared round the rocks.

'He'll find us,' said Sprout. 'Let's go.'

We abandoned the trolley and set off. Sprout scuttled up like a spider, but I didn't find it easy climbing up the steep rock face. Soon my fingers and knees were sore from gripping and knocking against the hard rock. I was getting very hot and my hair was falling in my eyes.

At last we reached a wide ledge and hauled ourselves on to it. We sat there panting, gazing back across the land. In the far distance we could see our forest home. I wondered if my parents had noticed I was missing yet. Probably not. I'd be home long before they got round to checking if I was awake. They'd never believe I was hundreds of tree-lengths away, perched on top of a huge rock.

I looked round. We were leaning against a wall made of large stones. I stood up and peered over. Behind the wall was a shimmering carpet of blue, sparkling water.

CHAPTER EIGHT

'Look,' I gasped. 'Here's all the water!'

Sprout scrambled to his feet and looked at the water which lay flat and still, surrounded by tall, jagged rocks.

'No wonder our trees are dying,' he said. 'Someone's blocked off the whole waterfall! Let's get rid of this wall!'

I pulled at one of the stones. Sprout helped, but we couldn't budge it. I cupped my hands and desperately started sloshing the water over the wall, trying to start the waterfall flowing again.

'That's no good,' sighed Sprout. 'You've just made our feet wet. Where's your uncle got to? He might have an invention that will help.'

'None of his others have been any use!' I scoffed, kicking frantically at the wall.

'Stop that!' came a heavy voice.

We looked up. Standing on the wall was a huge figure. He was like nothing I'd ever seen – or even imagined in my stories. He had great folds of green skin, and tiny yellow eyes that stared at us angrily. He was wearing a tunic and a round hat made of shiny metal, and in his pudgy hand he held a stick with spikes poking out of the end. He waved the stick threateningly at us.

'Big Blocker won't like this!' he growled.

'Big Blocker?' said Sprout faintly. 'Who's he?'

'You don't know who Big Blocker is?' gasped the guard, his folds of skin quivering with horror. 'He's king of us Plugs – may his blubber always wobble. He had this wall built specially to protect the water in his lake and I'm here, as head guard, to guard it.'

'I don't care who he is!' I shouted. I was too angry to be frightened. 'He can't pinch our water. *We* need it. The trees in our forest are dying.'

To my surprise the guard's face fell.

'Oh dear,' he said, scratching his head. 'That's a shame.'

'Isn't it,' said Sprout. 'So why don't you run along and ask your Big Blocker to give us our water back.'

'Good idea,' nodded the guard, grinning a dim, flabby grin. 'I'll pop off and see him now … Wait a minute. I'm a guard! Guards don't run along with messages! Guards strut up and down and guard things. Oh yes, and take prisoners. Men, arrest these creatures.'

Suddenly the ledge was full of blubbery Plug guards, all dressed alike. They herded us along a narrow stony path between the lake and the jagged rocks, poking us in the back with their spiky sticks. We came to an opening in the rock face. Water from the lake was spilling into it and the path followed.

We looked round desperately for Great-uncle Runnicles but there was still no sign of him. My ears began to flap with fear.

Without a word the guards pushed us through the opening and down a gloomy track lit by spluttering lamps. We stumbled along, deeper and deeper inside the rock, with the water flowing beside us. Now we could see an archway ahead and through it a bright yellow glow.

We were pushed into a huge cave. It was unbearably hot. In the middle was a bubbling pool with steam rising from it. Around the poolside were fires, with pots of boiling water on top. A bunch of sweating guards was frantically shovelling wood on to the fires.

In the middle of the water wallowed an enormous creature. He had the same blubbery skin and beady yellow eyes as the guards. But he was twice their size. He slowly turned and stared at us, sending huge waves over the side of the pool, making the fires hiss.

'What have you got there, Corporal Bung?' he asked lazily. His voice was deep and echoing, as if he was hollow inside.

'May your blubber always wobble, oh Big Blocker,' said the guard nervously. 'We found these strange creatures by the dam.'

'Well don't bother me with them!' Big Blocker sank deeper into his pool. 'More hot water, you lazy lollopers!' he ordered. The guards rushed forwards with their pots and poured the steaming water into the pool.

I took a deep breath and stepped forward. 'You've got to unplug the waterfall, Mr Blocker!' I demanded. 'Our forest is dying because the trees are not getting any of its water.'

Big Blocker looked at me in horror.

'Unplug the waterfall!' he bellowed. 'Never! For years I have searched the land for a wallowing place. And each time I found one it ran dry or got infested with frogs or made me itch. But now at last I have found my Perfect Plughole and I am going to keep it! I need every drop of water for it. How could I wallow without my lovely water?'

'They were trying to let your lovely water out, oh Big Blocker,' explained Corporal Bung helpfully.

The king of the Plugs opened his huge mouth.

'So that's why the water level dropped by an ant's whisker!' he roared. 'Guards – more bubbles! I need soothing.'

Three guards jumped forwards and blew hard down tubes into the water. Bubbles gurgled round the pool and Big Blocker lay back and closed his eyes.

'Please let the waterfall flow again,' pleaded Sprout. 'If the trees die our cities will be destroyed.'

Big Blocker's beady yellow eyes opened like a shot.

'As you're so interested in the waterfall,' he said, 'I know exactly how to help.' He turned to the head guard. 'Take them back there and chuck them off the top.'

'You can't throw us off the waterfall!' I shouted.

'She's right, Corporal Bung,' said Big Blocker, his blubbery lips curling in a nasty smile. 'You can't throw them off the waterfall.' He heaved himself out of the pool with a deafening gloop. 'Not till I'm there to see it!'

CHAPTER NINE

We stood on the waterfall ledge. The ground looked a long way away. It lurched and swayed before my eyes. Surely Big Blocker wasn't really going to have us pushed off. This was just a nasty game. The guards struggled to get their king comfortable on the wall, heaving at his blubber so none of it was hanging in the cold water behind him.

Sprout and I wriggled and kicked against Corporal Bung but it was no use. He had us firmly in his hefty fists. Then Sprout suddenly stopped struggling.

'Seems to me you do all the work round here, Corporal Bung,' he said.

'I certainly do,' answered the guard proudly.

'This is no time for a chat,' I hissed. But Sprout carried on.

'I bet you guards never get a go in the pool.'

'No,' said Corporal Bung sadly, 'though we always wear swimming trunks under our armour just in case. Only Big Blocker – may his blubber always wobble – goes in the pool.'

'How unfair!' said Sprout.

Corporal Bung let go of us and scratched his green forehead thoughtfully.

Now I realised what Sprout had been up to. Slowly, we began to back away from the edge. He didn't notice and the other guards were still busy arranging Big Blocker's flab on the wall. But before we could escape there was a shout from below and a head popped up over the ledge. Big Blocker was so surprised he fell backwards into the lake, covering us all in icy water.

It was Great-uncle Runnicles! He hoisted himself on to the ledge.

'Where did you two get to?' he panted. He had a coil of creeper rope slung over his shoulder and one end was tied round his waist. He looked round at the guards who were hauling their furious king out of the lake. 'Hello there! Need some help?'

'Bung!' spluttered Big Blocker as he flopped back on to the wall. 'Don't let them escape! Throw them off the ledge – and him too!'

'We haven't got time to be thrown off ledges,' said Great-uncle Runnicles. 'We've got a waterfall to find!' He strolled over to Big Blocker. 'Listen chummy,' he said, 'if you dare throw me to my death, I'll come back and haunt you.'

'Don't care!' said Big Blocker.

'I'll be a very nasty ghost.'

'You don't scare me.'

'I'll keep popping up!'

'My guards won't let you,' he said. 'Fubsy, Paunch, throw him off.'

Two guards moved forwards menacingly.

'Have it your own way,' said Great-uncle Runnicles cheerfully. He held out the end of his rope to the guards. 'Hold this for me, there's good chaps.'

Fubsy and Paunch obediently took the rope. And without waiting to be pushed, Great-uncle Runnicles stepped off the edge of the waterfall.

Sprout and I were frozen to the spot. Great-uncle Runnicles had jumped to his death!

'That was easy!' grunted Big Blocker. 'Now for you two ...' He broke off as the figure of Great-uncle Runnicles suddenly appeared in the air above the ledge.

'Beware!' it moaned before it disappeared back down.

A second later it reappeared.

'I'll haunt you ...' it wailed and disappeared again.

'... for ever!' it howled as it disappeared for the third time.

The guards stood open-mouthed and

Fubsy and Paunch dropped the rope.

'Excuse me, oh Big Blocker, may your blubber always wobble,' said Corporal Bung anxiously, 'but that ghost says he's going to haunt you for ever.'

'He wouldn't dare!' snarled Big Blocker. 'Chuck these two off, then get back and stoke up the fires. You'll keep the plughole nice and hot if it's the last thing you do.'

But Corporal Bung shook his head. 'Not going back there if it's haunted,' he said. 'And anyway I've been thinking. It's not fair. Us guards do all the work.'

'That's right!' muttered the guards. 'We do all the work.'

'Course you do,' snapped Big Blocker. 'You're guards!' He heaved himself off the wall and prodded Corporal Bung with a podgy finger. 'And guards do as I say!'

'Oh … sorry,' said Corporal Bung. 'I forgot. Guards do as you say, oh Big Blocker, may your blubber …'

'You don't have to follow his orders!' hissed Sprout.

'No we don't!' said Corporal Bung, happily. 'We don't have to follow your orders.'

'How dare you!' growled Big Blocker. 'Guards! Arrest that guard!'

But nobody moved. Big Blocker turned purple with rage and his blubber quivered violently. He shook his fists and stamped his foot in temper. The ledge shook.

'Obey me!' he screeched. The guards just stared at him.

Big Blocker paced angrily up and down the ledge. His blubber blobbed from side to side and his feet thundered on the rock. Small cracks appeared under him and snaked across to the wall.

'Excuse me, oh Big Blocker,' said Corporal Bung politely, 'but I think you ought to stop hopping about.'

'Nobody tells me what to do!' shrieked Big Blocker.

The cracks had reached the wall.

'Everyone off the ledge!' I shouted. 'The wall's going to break!'

The guards slowly backed away to the safety of the pathway. Sprout and I followed.

Big Blocker pointed a furious finger at us.

'This is all your fault,' he bellowed. 'You'll be sorry you crossed the king of the Plugs. I'm going to throw you off myself.'

He lumbered heavily towards us. We turned to run and smacked into a clump of dithering guards. There was no way past. We were trapped.

But the stones in the wall were moving. Water was beginning to trickle through the cracks. And as Big Blocker's gigantic hands reached out to grab us, the water burst through the wall with an almighty roar. Big Blocker was bowled clean off his feet and disappeared over the ledge.

The water tumbled down the rock face and fell with a loud splash into the dip in the ground, making a huge, bubbling pool. At once a river began to weave its way from it, across the land towards the trees in our forest. The guards cheered and waved their sticks. Sprout and I hugged each other. The Waterfall of Wonderful Wetness was flowing again!

CHAPTER TEN

Sprout and I scrambled down the rocks at the side of the waterfall. The guards followed. When they reached the bubbling pool at the bottom they tossed their sticks to the ground and threw off their armour. Dressed in a variety of brightly coloured swimming trunks, they leapt into the pool. Corporal Bung stood on the bank in pink and yellow stripes, grinning broadly.

'This is better than that stupid plughole,' he said. 'It was hard work boiling up all that water and this pool makes its own bubbles.' Then his face fell. 'But I'll miss being a guard.'

'You can still be a guard,' said Sprout. 'If you all stay here you can guard the waterfall – and wallow as much as you want!'

'You're right!' exclaimed Corporal Bung. And he jumped in with a huge splash.

Sprout and I sat on the edge of the pool.

'Suppose we'd better get back,' I said. 'The water's flowing. Our cities are safe.'

'We should be celebrating,' said Sprout miserably.

'Don't feel like it,' I muttered. 'Poor Uncle Runnicles. He came to a bad end after all.'

'Did I?' said a voice behind us.

Great-uncle Runnicles was standing there with his trolley and his twig! I flung my arms round him.

'You're alive!' I gasped.

'Course I am!' he exclaimed. 'I had my elastic creeper round my waist when I jumped so I pinged straight back up. I call it bouncy jumping. I'd still be bouncing now if those silly guards hadn't let go of my rope. Luckily I landed in a bush.' He suddenly noticed the water crashing over the rocks. 'Jumping tree-frogs – there's the waterfall! I knew I'd find it in the end!'

Sprout and I looked at each other.

'Well done, Uncle Runnicles!' we said.

Then we heard a strange groaning. The guards were cowering in the pool and pointing at Great-uncle Runnicles.

'It's the ghost!' they gibbered.

'Indeed,' wailed Great-uncle Runnicles, flapping his arms. 'Leave this pool immediately and never return.'

'No, Uncle Runnicles,' I hissed, pulling at his tunic. 'We want them to stay and guard the pool.'

'You do?'

'Yes, it's very important!'

'Righty-ho.' Great-uncle Runnicles turned back to the guards. 'Change of plan. You are to stay and guard the pool. I will return to make sure you do.'

Ten minutes later we were sailing in Great-uncle Runnicles' trolley down the river that ran from the waterfall towards our forest. Great-uncle Runnicles sat in the back, lost in his book. It was only when we got near the forest we realised we were in big trouble. Ahead of us the river disappeared into the ground.

'We've got to get out!' I yelled.

Sprout and I grabbed Uncle Runnicles and we threw ourselves on to the riverbank as the trolley was sucked underground.

'Crumbling conifers!' exclaimed Great-uncle Runnicles, fanning himself with his book. 'So that's why the Rootles didn't know about the river. It flows under Rootstock!'

We ran through the forest. We couldn't wait to tell everybody how we'd saved the trees.

When we got to Rootstock we found a tall metal ladder at the edge of the clearing. It reached high into the trees and the top of the ladder was hidden among the branches. Rootles were scuttling around excitedly at the bottom.

'What's happening?' said Sprout.

'Chief's gone to sort out those tree-people,' snapped a passing Rootle.

'To stop them throwing branches,' said another.

'We've got to get up there fast!' I exclaimed. 'Come on, Uncle Runnicles.'

We'd settle this in no time. Once everyone heard about the waterfall we'd be heroes. We began to climb the ladder – it seemed to go on forever. Great-uncle Runnicles struggled up behind us, clutching his soggy old book.

At last Sprout and I reached the top. We were in the middle of Skyville! Sprout's dad and a bunch of angry-looking Rootles were on the walkway outside Mrs Sycamore's shop, shouting at Mayor Crabapple and the quivering Elders.

'Stop throwing branches at us or there'll be war!' Chief Rootle was yelling.

'We never throw branches!' exclaimed Mayor Crabapple indignantly. 'They are falling because you are killing our trees and we wish you to stop. We will be sending down a bark letter to tell you so.'

'Any excuse to drop things on us!' snapped Sprout's dad. He stepped forwards and shook his fist in the mayor's face.

'Stop!' I cried.

Everyone turned and stared.

'No one's to blame,' I said, as Sprout and I climbed over the wall on to the walkway. 'The trees were dying because the Waterfall of Wonderful Wetness had stopped flowing. But we've unplugged it and our cities are saved.' I looked round waiting for the applause. But no one clapped.

'Lia Vine!' said the mayor, appalled. 'I hope you have not been down below the leaves with these dreadful ground-dwellers!'

'You can't fool us, Mayor,' exclaimed Chief Rootle. 'We know you sent her.' He poked a finger at Sprout. 'And you're in big trouble, boy. You let her out of the cage.'

'You locked Lia up?' gasped Mayor Crabapple, his ears flapping with horror.

Everybody started shouting again.

'Wiggling weevils!' came a voice, and my great-uncle clambered up beside us.

'Runnicles Juniper!' said Mayor Crabapple in astonishment. 'We never thought to see you again after you disappeared in your dreadful mechanical bus!'

'He tried to blow up Rootstock!' said Chief Rootle. 'He's dangerous, like all tree-people. Glad we kicked you lot out of Rootstock all that time ago.'

'You did not kick us out,' said Mayor Crabapple. 'We left because you … did something dreadful.'

'Rubbish!' shouted Chief Rootle. 'It was you lot who were the dreadful ones!'

'What happened?' asked Sprout.

The mayor and Chief Rootle eyed each other cautiously.

I grinned. 'You don't know, do you!'

'I do!' Great-uncle Runnicles chipped in, waving his book. 'It's all in here. I think it will amuse you. Our ancestors found a great waterfall that gave life to all our trees. They were so impressed they vowed to give it its own sign so everyone should know that this was the Waterfall of Wonderful Wetness. But they could not agree about the words for the sign. So they split into two groups and put up two signs. One group sulked on the ground and the other group flounced off in a huff to live in the trees. Isn't that a hoot!'

Nobody laughed.

'So that's all it was!' I said. 'Our ancestors couldn't agree about the words on a sign! You should be ashamed of yourselves carrying on a silly, unimportant quarrel!'

The Rootles shuffled their feet with embarrassment and the Skylers' noses drooped.

'Now perhaps you'll listen to me,' I said severely.

And I told them all about our adventure.

'… so you don't have to argue any more,' I finished. 'Our trees are safe and Uncle Runnicles will visit the guards to make sure they are doing their job.'

Mayor Crabapple frowned. 'We cannot leave such an important task to him,' he said doubtfully.

'You're right,' said Chief Rootle. 'He's such an oddbud!'

'I agree,' nodded the mayor. 'I intend to go with him and see this waterfall for myself.'

'Good idea!' said Sprout's dad. 'We'll set off straightaway.'

'But we shall need time to prepare …'

'Five minutes then?'

Sprout and I left them arguing over their plans for the journey. We had plans of our own. We were going to do something the Lia in my stories had never done. We were going bouncy jumping.